Bloodstone Institute

David Dugas Jr

Copyright © 2016 David Dugas Jr

All rights reserved.

ISBN: 10-**1533124779**
ISBN-13-**978-1533124777**

DEDICATION

This story is completely fiction with somethings being told by past volunteers of their own personal paranormal experience. All characters are based from real volunteers in a fictional form. It was said that the real Chinchuba was haunted, I experienced somethings myself to believe it was in fact haunted. This story is dedicated to all the volunteers and friends from Chinchuba Haunted House, and to all the good souls that we lost over the years. These were the best years of my life that I will never forget. I met some wonderful people, learned some interesting things, most of all we were family and never forgotten. This place made me who I am today, it kept me away from doing bad things, thankfully nothing never followed me home from there LOL. I wanted to do this story as a dedication to the best time of my life, to the greatest family in the world. I hope who and if anyone from there ever reads this you will enjoy it and bring back memories of your own. I enjoyed writing a fictional story with a fictional background on what we use to call home. For the Chinchuba cast and school, I thank you for inspiring me to write this story and for letting me be a part of the haunted house. It is forever in my blood, my passion and my thoughts. Farewell my Chinchuba family.

David Dugas Jr aka Rufus.

ACKNOWLEDGMENTS

I want to thank my author writing friends, who have helped me through this and guided me. Brandon, Emily, April, Christian and Shelly. I want to thank my friends who have read some of my pre-work and helped me get better at this. I want to thank my mind that has been full of imagination since I was a kid. I want to thank Erica the love of my life who puts up with me every day, I love you. Last, I want to thank John Brown and Sasha Klanott who helped me start the ball on getting this first story self-published. Anybody else I left, friends and family there is too many of you, I love you all and thank you for everything.

Prologue

Decades of a living hell. That is the purgatory left to one building with a name. It was 1950, the Archdiocese of New Orleans and Sisters of the Notre Dame opened the first school devoted to teaching children of the hearing impaired. The school was known as Hope Institute, named after a quote from Archbishop Francis Jansen. The exterior of the building was Spanish masonry painted all satin white with dark green trim around the door and window frames. The inside was remodeled as decades passed, eventually included a small cafeteria for the students to eat with a decent size kitchen for the cooking, a hall that lead to a stairway to the second floor with five classrooms.

It was ran first by Archbishop Francis who later passed away in his bed peacefully. The institute was passed from torch to torch in the years after first being started. Eventually ran by nuns that looked like day ghost roaming around in their all white uniforms.

The most bizarre years began around 1962 during the Vietnam War. It was ran by thirty-year-old Sister Elizabeth Foret. She would become more arrogant and threatening after her secretive husband Jonathan T. Coleman came back from the war. With him being African American, their marriage was kept secret cause of the time of segregation. And because she was a nun. Nuns were not allowed to wed because of their religion. No one would dare cross Sister Elizabeth, especially with her new behavior.

In 1970 police get a call. Inside what they see stays in their dreams for the rest of their lives. Innocent deaf children, nun's, Sister Elizabeth, and Jonathan all dead in a puddle of blood. The scene was so disturbing many officers turned away puking their guts out. The center image of the scene was the blood. Officers said the blood was splattered and colored like the Bloodstone colors on a heliotrope rock, giving the institute the nick name, Bloodstone Institute.

From the time Sister Elizabeth went mad up to the present, the building has been changed around with personnel. There have been records of deaths and people scared away because of strange happenings, along with rumors of ghost stories inside the institute. The school went into a drought for almost a decade after the murders. No one wanted to send their kids to the site of a blood bath school massacre, but it was the only local school for the deaf. To get more students in the school, decreasing the finances to send a student there was the only way to succeed. The stories continue inside Bloodstone Institute or the real name Hope Institute, where the Archbishop once said. "The building of hope, where faith lingers, and evil vanishes. It is the hope, prayer and time we face to heal our wounds and bless ourselves for all we are."

Now the school runs with a leg barely left to stand. A seasonal haunted house fundraiser, the heart and soul in the finances helps keep it alive. People quitting or getting hurt still. Only evil and mystery remand inside the institute, preying on new people who dare to challenge it.

The year is now 1995. A decade rumors of the school closing and still sitting on its last leg by a miracle. People point at the school as they pass by, calling it the spook house being of its history and now a money making haunted attraction. They doomed them as a freak show for making money on the side with creatures lurking the interior walls. And doom them from the dark history that they seem to forget and move forward as an attraction.

Denise Barrios was in her mid-twenties; she had taken the job because no other schools would hire her without a Degree. She was staring deep into the clock on the wall, tick tock, tick tock. All she could do was twirl her long brown hair with her fingers while reading one of her erotic novels. She was ready for the day to end, she can hear the sounds from outside of children playing in the playground and John aka old man Clements cutting the grass. The inside of the school was calm and silent throughout the halls. The classrooms smelled of fresh cleanness from the soap and spray. Denise has had some strange experiences since being at Hope Institute for a year, with all the dark history behind the walls. Why something strange wouldn't happen?

She has told the other administrators about the sounds she hears, the feeling of being watched and the fragrance she constantly smells. All they do is laugh and say the same thing, "I've been here for years and haven't had anything weird happen to me." She felt like the red haired step child knowing she experiences things that they don't. Deep down Denise felt that some or most of the other administrators have felt and sensed the same things as her, but don't want to admit it for fear that they will be embarrassed and called crazy. Denise did not believe in ghost or spirits, but was aware that what she was experiencing in the school was not normal and not human like. Only science can debunk things and make sense to us, other things are just too unpredictable and have no answers for its cause.

Denise was still single, looking for the perfect man that can give her the world. She constantly dreamed and thought about getting her true prince, but working at the school was like being trapped in purgatory. The school operates from ten in the morning till three in the afternoon with a thirty-minute lunch followed by recess on the playground. By the time she gets home, she is to exhausted for a night out looking for someone and with the stories of being watched in an old school is a laughing stock to another man who doesn't believe in that type of superstition. The children take their time learning to speak, but the school gets good results from a group of patient talented teachers and administration.

The school was connected to an older part of the building that is now used for a "haunted" attraction, they called Bloodstone Institute, named after the nickname the school has been branded with since the 1970 murders. The attraction was brought up by a former Director of the school Virginia Anderson in 1988 when the school was sitting on its last leg with finance problems. Her husband Edward a construction worker, came up with the idea for a haunted house during October while reading through a handbook on charities. The attraction was the bread and butter to keeping the school alive and a hangout for friends and family that would create a new door for fun. Denise never went in that part of the school. She never liked horror movies or Halloween. As long as money was coming from it and it was ran by a good group of leaders, she stayed out the way. She was asked sometimes to go over there for something, but she would fine a wondering volunteer outside and hand them the task.

It was lunch time, Denise ate her turkey sandwich in her office. The sound of calm went to a sound of a little girl giggling. "Is there anyone there?" She asked with no reply and no one in the building. She walked slowly out her office into the hallway calling for anybody to answer back. Again, a giggle echoed across the hall. She ran towards the sound only to find nothing or no one. She paused to look around the hall. Then out of nowhere the giggle came from down the stairs. She began to walk slowly on the first step listening for anything. "Hello is there anyone there?" She asked, walking one step down. She felt a presence force push her from behind. Her body rolled down the steps as she screamed on the way down busting her head open and breaking her neck. Her body laid there for ten minutes before recess was over. The children and teachers entered to the stairs to her soulless body lying at the bottom of the stairs in her own puddle of blood. Death by accident or death by act of rage from the unknown?

Part 1
1995

Chapter 1

Two months passed since the freak accident of Denise at Hope Institute. Police questioned everybody, they knew a silent mystery existed in that school, but could never find an answer. The cops did not worry about leads and knew the chief would ignore the situation. Ever since the nickname Bloodstone Institute, the local cops try to avoid the school as much as possible.

    The search for Denise's replacement dragged on without notice until LSU graduate Dominoe Breaux stepped up for the position. She was a twenty-four-year-old graduate with a Masters and Associates in general studies, education and business. She sat in the main office waiting nervously, constantly checking her makeup in her pocket mirror and fixing her curly blonde hair. She was applying for Denise's replacement as Executive Director of the institute. Mr. Mike Harville, the hiring manager of the school, made his way into the office. She heard he was a demanding and intimidating man, intimidating was right on. He was tall and slim with a serious personality. He kept asking her question's that really makes you think twice before answering. The interview process went on for an hour leaving her with a massive headache and an impatient answer to where her career stands. She had a goal in life which was to pay off any school debts and make a decent amount to live life the fullest.

Dominoe walked out of the building feeling a chill run down her spine as she turned around looking at the building in the distance. There was something about this place deep down, but the pay and benefits was hard to refuse. She drove back to her small shot gun house off Salia Ave in Westwego, twenty minutes outside of New Orleans. It was given to her parents when her grandparents died. Instead of selling they gave it to her as a big graduation present. It needed a little up to date work but was livable and a roof over her head. One long hallway lead to all the rooms in the house. The walls were dark plum purple and gold trim. She cleaned it once a week, cooked every night, read and did writing on the side as a hobby.

Two days went by finally she received a call back from Mr. Harville offering her the Executive Director position. She was so excited, she couldn't stop jumping up and down. She was starting in the morning and was to report directly to Maria Jones, the head of all the institute. A pizza delivery and wine were for dinner to celebrate, a smile on her face to last a lifetime.

It was a quiet, calm night. She laid in her bed tossing and turning. She was excited that her hard years of work and school had finally paid off. She was also glad to be part of a school that helps the disabled need as she has always had a passion for helping children. The only thing standing out in the back of her mind was that eerie feeling as she walked out and stared at the school. She couldn't let it bother her, she had a job, a good start in adulthood and a change coming.

The alarm went off, she jumped up in surprise slapping the top of her clock. Dominoe fixed her a cup of coffee while she waited for her toast. She placed three dresses on the bed, trying to decide what to wear on her first day. She finally decides to wear the white button shirt and black skirt with her black high heels.

She pulled into the school in her yellow bug staring up at the tallness of the building and its outside old features. She got out of her car walking up to the school looking deep at it seeing that it has not been repainted in quite a long time. The growth of vines and weeds outside, fading white with brownish stains on it. She was startled by the maintenance guy, old man Clements. "I'm so sorry my dear I did not mean to startle you like that." He said in a deep Cajun accent. She held her hand to her heart breathing deep. "That's OK, can you tell me where Ms. Maria is?" "Yes, mam go through the front glass French doors up the stairs first office to the left." "Thank you so much."

Dominoe walked around looking into the fog faded windows feeling eerie of this building. She wanted to exam parts of the school before a grand tour. She entered through the doors, up the steps and into the office. Ms. Maria was waiting inside with her brown hair in a ponytail. "Good morning Dominoe, so nice to have you part of our institute." She thanked her back with the wonderful greeting and had Maria show her around the school. She was stunned and unaware of their haunted attraction. She was no fan of ghost and goblins, but once Maria explained the attraction she was on board with the idea and liked that they could raise money once a year to help keep the school. The Archdiocese did not give the school a lot of pocket change to help them, because of the history and lack of student increase. The haunted attraction raised thousands in one month that holds up and keeps the school running, old man Clements was once going to get let go but agreed on a price decrease to stay cause of his age. Dominoe was not interested in the tour of the attraction, especially since they were building and setting up for the new season.

It was August with just a few months before the haunt opened and a fresh new school year. The building used for the attraction was an old part of the school connected. It was once closed cause of asbestos, they took the asbestos out to use the building for their charity yearly idea with the haunted house. The windows were all painted in black to cover up from people seeing the inside. The exterior brick was a yellow beige with green stain running down. To top the weirdness off there was a huge statue of the Virgin Mary in the middle of the cemented courtyard. It was once at the church where Archbishop Francis serviced in Covington, then moved at the institute as a tribute to him after his death. The crowd always questioned the statue at the haunted house, but no one dare judge or explain they just say it's part of the graveyard scene they set up around it to try and cover it up and go with the scene.

This building was very weird to Dominoe, after the tour she was questioning herself why and if she should be here, but would she get another chance at this opportunity. They were about to walk back inside the school as Dominoe stopped in the middle of the courtyard looking up at the third window from the top. She saw a nun looking down at her with a faded white pale face, but full body form. "Are you coming Dominoe?" She looked at Maria then looked back up, seeing the mysterious nun vanished from the window. "Yes, I'm coming right behind you Ms. Maria." She walked off startled staring at the same window and to the other windows not seeing anything. Was she imagining this or was there a crazy nun inside the school waiting for someone or something she thought?

Chapter 2

After being shown around, Dominoe and Ms. Maria walked back into the office. Dominoe immediately went to work looking at school records and financial reports. She spent about an hour and a half going through everything, even finding a box full of old bloodstone institute haunted house shirts that dated back to its original opening year. There was also a lot of junk from old boxes that she tossed away that was no need to be there. Dominoe stopped and began to walk around looking at all closets and closed in spaces to see if there was anyone hiding. She still had the image of that mysterious nun she saw in the window. She was still confused at what she saw.

After looking and finding nothing she sat down to eat her usual healthy lunch. A grilled chicken salad with a blueberry granola bar for dessert. She was feasting while flipping through old pictures of the school. She noticed the changes from the building and was amazed to study how it's done all these years. She was just about finished when she saw a newspaper of a suicide dated from March 18, 1967. It was a nun named Pam O'

Flynn. It wasn't the story that made her pause with a pale look, it was the picture in the article. The picture was the same nun; she saw in the window in the courtyard. Is this school haunted by spirits she thought? She slammed the book closed shut and pronounced it as nonsense, this is reality. She did not believe in ghost. She was catholic and believed in God, heaven and hell, but questioned the man called Satan.

It was three in the afternoon and school was done for the day. Dominoe was exhausted from her first full day as Executive Director. She walked out the school with her briefcase. She had a sudden urge to browse and check the other part of the school where the haunted house was. She walked to the exterior of the building slowly, she was greeted at the door by one of the volunteer workers. It was a three-hundred-pound Spanish dark skin man named Mongo. He looked intimidating with his full beard, mustache and stood six feet tall. He showed her inside giving a tour. The entrance was all chamber like sets painted gray and black that led to the very first scene called the angel of death. Inside was a guillotine and a basket filled with fake heads, gates painted black with red spot lights pointing down to the set with a bell sound through the speakers. The tour continued as she saw all kinds of other rooms including a psycho ward, meat locker, chainsaw scene, electric chair room that the fans called shocker, alien scene, rag hallway, clown room nick named Creepo, the famous black out maze that the customer came back every year for and many more. She was disturbed by all the scenes and how detailed they were and how dark each room was even with white lights on.

Mongo left her to go finish painting black walls, she began to walk back to the front when she stopped from the sound of a bouncing ball and a little girl screaming like she was playing with it in the hallway. "Hello?" She asked walking slowly to the back of the haunt. She saw no one but heard the same noises. She startled Mongo asking if he heard or seen anyone? "We are the only two people in here right now senorita," he replied confusedly. "Thank you, Mongo," she replied with a smile walking as fast as she can out to the cast room and into the exit door. She ran to her car in total fear and pulled her car around to the back of the courtyard staring at the haunted house part of the school with mystery and chills running through her body. She backed up driving slowly around the courtyard to leave. She slammed on her breaks looking up. Once again, she saw the mysterious nun in the window looking down at her in the courtyard. She peeled off from the school looking at it through the rear window wondering if she should come back or not.

Chapter 3

Dominoe drove home with that nun's face in her head. She slapped herself trying to erase the image but couldn't. Her hands were shaking on the wheel and her arms full of goosebumps. She was startled by the car honking behind her, looking up seeing the light had turned green and she was daydreaming.

She arrived at her house very startled by the events at the school. She was ready to just not show back up but needed the money and it was her first career to build a resume. She had a life, bills and financial aid that needed to be paid off, running out the school like that would look bad.   The sun finally went down as she got in the shower bathing in her cupcake scented body wash. She placed her head underneath the warm shower humming songs to herself with her eyes closed. She stopped the water after hearing a crash sound from the kitchen that sounded like glass shattering. She listened for any sound or movement. "Hello?" She walked out the shower in her baby blue bathrobe and began to walk slowly hearing only the sound of her wet bare feet squash the wood panel floor. "If anybody is there I'm going to call the cops!" She walked into the living room slowly, placing her hand over her gasp mouth staring at the ground. One of her glass dark red candle covers was shattered on the floor. The candle holder was made of metal, for the cover to just fall on the ground some kind of force had to push it, grab it, or drop it. No wind or loose handle in the wall could cause the incident. She was puzzled of this and freaked out. She picked up the pieces of glass off the floor looking around still seeing no one inside. Goosebumps popped out all over her arm with her hairs standing straight up. Her body shook, wet drops fell to the floor from her blonde wet hair.

    Dominoe laid in her bed looking up at the ceiling thinking about her day. She still did not believe in ghost but could not explain to herself of what was happening. It was two in the morning, she was sound asleep, when a slight cold breeze waved through her curly blonde hair. She pulled out her key chain flashlight to look around the room. She waved it back and forth, seeing in the corner of her eye a small dark shadow passing her bedroom into the hallway. She stood up out of her bed running in the hallway to turn on the hall light. She walked around the house looking but found nothing. She walked back to her bedroom rubbing her head with exhaustion as she crawled back to bed, placing her head down, taking deep breaths until she went back to sleep to prepare for her next morning of whatever happens.

Chapter 4

The Morning came sooner than expected. Dominoe sat at the kitchen table brewing her French press coffee while eating a red apple. She got dressed in her long gray button shirt and black dress pants. She wore her green diamond necklace her mom gave her graduation. The same green that matched her pretty green eyes. She looked at her hand, watching it shake and began to feel nervous. She closed her eyes to say a prayer slowly to herself then opened them taking a deep breath, feeling calmer.

She got into her car driving off to work. She arrived and began to walk to the front of the school. She stopped before entering as a homeless man approached her. He was very old age, wearing a dark faded short sleeve green shirt, blue jeans and beige boots. The smell coming from him was pure disgusting, his long white beard was stained with God knows what, he raised his hand pointing at her. "Your doom, you're going to die like she did, like the others did. This school is cursed you hear me cursed!" Old man Clements came out of nowhere, grabbing the homeless man, "get out of here Andy and leave this lady alone or

I'll call the cops!" The homeless man ran off screaming along the way "cursed, cursed, cursed!" "Are you OK Ms. Dominoe?" "Yes sir, I'm fine. What did he mean cursed and something about the other lady?" Old man Clements paused placing his hand on his white mustache rubbing it. "There was a freak accident with the lady before you. She fell down the steps breaking her neck, as for the curse. There is a dark history of this school, so dark that it's too disturbing to talk about. If you want to know more about it, I suggest you research it young lady but beware you won't find any happy endings here." He walked away with his rake over his right shoulder as she did not know about any dark past. When she was younger, she heard of people going into this school and not coming out but knew they wouldn't keep a school running if that really happened. She never thought twice about the silly stories, she just let it all go through one ear and out the other.

    Dominoe sat at her desk in the middle of the afternoon, it was lunch time. Ms. Maria came in with her brown hair brushed back, to see how things were going. After a small talk Dominoe stopped her to ask. "Is this place haunted?" Maria paused and turned around with a silent voice from what she just heard. "No mam granted some weird stuff happens around here it's just cause the school and building is so old it's like past things are planted here like a photograph." She walked away with a smile like she was hiding something or knew about Dominoes question was true and did not want to admit it.

    The end of the day came as she walked down the stairs looking at the steps in disbelief that someone fell and died right here recently. She walked out the school seeing a bunch of construction workers heading to the other building to do more work. "Hello," Chip said to her. He was a bald headed pale skin slim young adult. One of the oldest volunteers there. Dominoe turned around startled by five nine David shaking her hand, then scratching his scruffy brown-haired face. Then Damon the black male tour guide of the attraction shook her hand while whipping dust off his mustache. They were all nice to her, holding a beer in one hand and wood in the other. "Have any of you guys ever experienced anything weird along the walls of the haunted house?" They all looked at her taking a sip of their beer as Chip looked at her and the guys. "We have to get to work, still have a lot to do before the season starts. It was nice to meet you." They all walked off with their beer and tools. She believed they knew something, but not telling her, no one seemed to speak of anything odd that went on around there.

    She got in her car, driving ten minutes to Manhattan Boulevard. She entered the Jefferson Parish Library to check out books as research. She didn't believe in things of the unknown but needed hard proof that she wasn't crazy and that there was the possibility of the unknown. She gathered what she needed, then headed home hoping to find answers and something about the school.

Chapter 5

She arrived home placing her book bag down, going straight to her computer. She got online to research the school and past murder cases in that area. She paused as she was about to type in Hope Institute and decided that faith of her knowing of what she doesn't know is best kept away for right now. She instead turned her computer off and walked away from it.

She kicked her shoes off and laid on the couch with a glass of red wine while reading the books she checked out about the paranormal. Some things she read she was experiencing like the sounds, ghost possibly following her home, shadow figures, cold breeze and the sight of the nun as a full apparition form. What also struck her interest and curiosity was the description of a malevolent spirit, on how negative and dangerous it can be. The thought of this type of spirit was bringing her back to earlier hearing about the girl who fell down the stairway. The slip resistance steps are very wide to walk up and down on. Could a malevolent spirit have gotten enough energy to push her down the stairs, making it look like an accident?

She went online looking up paranormal cases and stories.

She found stories of people claiming to have been scratched, bitten and shoved. The goosebumps were rising on her arms; her hair was pointing straight up again. She started reading about how you catch a spirit's voice through an EVP or recorder. She placed her glass of wine down and left the computer. She began going through her drawer to find her old tape recorder from college and a tape in it. If she can catch a noise or spirit on tape, maybe then she will be convinced for the first time in her life about something she has never believed in or ever imagined believing in.

She walked back to the computer, reading reviews about a local medium named Stephanie Ariel. She had been known to speak to ghost since she was six years old and can communicate with them very well. With all three books she checked out from the library she had a small, but enough knowledge to keep an open mind for unknown things.

She pulled out her grandma's cross from the funeral that was blessed and began going around, her house saying the Saint Michael prayer that she studied in one of the books.

"Saint Michael the Archangel, defend us in battle, be our

protection against the wickedness and snares of the devil. May God rebuke him we humbly pray, and do you, O prince of the heavenly host, by the power of God thrust into hell Satan and all the evil spirits who prowl about the world seeking the ruin of souls. Amen."

There was no sign of negative spirits, just the one incident with the shadow, but she felt better saying the prayer. It couldn't hurt anything only make her comfort better and her house safer. She spent hours reading and began to creep herself out, but her brain was full of things like she was back in school. She tossed the books to the side and picked up the rest of her wine. It was time for her evening shower and bed time. On to another day at Bloodstone Institute.

Chapter 6

It was the middle of a humid August making it feel like a hundred degrees with clear skies. Dominoe sat at her desk, staring at the tape recorder like she wanted it to talk right back at her that second. The second floor was quiet and clear with all the teachers and students in the playground. Old man Clements was weeding the garden; Ms. Maria was gone for the day for a doctor appointment.

Dominoe got up from her chair and began to walk slowly down the hallway. She entered the classes with the tape recorder on. "Hi, my name is Dominoe, is there anyone here?" No sound or echo came from the rooms. "Is there anybody here with me? If there is someone here can you say something into the tape recorder in my hand? Can you make something move, throw something at me?" She then heard a toy piano playing for a second in the next room. She ran to the room seeing nothing there. She sat down on top one of the small student desk and replayed her tape hearing her own voice in the replay. She rewinded the tape and stopped it. She pressed play, hearing a voice she did not hear in the room. It was a little girl's voice she can barely make out. "I want to play," it said softly. She replayed the tape, then kept rolling to listen to repeated voices saying. "Help me Ms." What did it mean help me? It could have been from a malevolent spirit that she was sure caused the death of the girl that worked there now.

She heard books falling on the floor. She hurried to the next classroom. There was a line of books on the floor like they had been thrown to the ground. She pulled her tape recorder out again, this time in a demanding voice. "If someone is here leave now! What do you want from me?! Talk to me now, in this recorder!" Then out of nowhere she heard a growling sound like a dog coming from behind her ear. She ran out of the classroom, sitting in the middle of the hallway replaying her tape recorder. She heard the growling noises louder and deeper like a monster than with a sentence following that scared her half to death. "You're going to die!" It said in an evil growly monstrous tone. She placed her hand over her mouth and began to cry and shake. She picked up her tape recorder and ran downstairs to be around people, being alone was the last thing on her mind.

Chapter 7

The green grass in the playground was like a golf course, it was so clean and fresh looking. The children played with laughter, the teachers watched, enjoying them having fun. Dominoe had the tape recorder in her pocket with the growling evil voice planted in her head. What was this thing doing there and why would it want to harm anybody? She remembered reading about evil entities and of how rare they can be. There is this talk about a dark evil past that circles this place and how it had affected people and the name itself all these years.

She remained silent the rest of the day about the encounter, everyone was in such a happy mood, no need to kill it. She was so frightened; she didn't have the guts to walk back to her office to get her things. She just left them there to return to on Monday. She watched some of the volunteer's goof off outside as she was walking to her car. For a spooky event, they made it look like Disneyland and had no shame in being the black sheep of all groups.

Dominoe got to her car, realizing her keys were in her bag upstairs. She slammed her head against the car crying, not wanting to go back into that evil building. She walked slowly back to the building, walking faster as she approached it. Without hesitation, she ran up the stairs to grab her bag, then back down, out the door and into her car. She was breathing fast sitting in her seat, staring at the school from her rear mirror once again. Her breathing slowed down while she was saying a prayer to herself. She turned the car on, drove off to go home.

It was four in the evening with traffic in Westwego cause of a wreck on the expressway. She couldn't wait any longer, so she cut to a side street to get to Fourth Street. She walked to the front of her house like a zombie, placing her stuff down inside, laying back on her chocolate colored sofa, pulling out the tape recorder. She replayed everything as she bit down on her nails. "You will die." She could not get the voice out her head.

She went back to her library books, looking again about the malevolent entities. Two ways of it occurring are evil spirits that have died there and refused to go to the other side, spreading pain to others and thrived over weak energy. The second was when groups perform seances that can bring any kind of spirit from a portal door the group opens because they have no control of what comes in and out of the gateway. Dominoe suddenly remembered she had a cousin who worked at the haunted house the first few years when it started for community hours and did not speak of it much, only scared her with ghost stories, so she would never go there. It was time for a phone call and possible family visit.

Chapter 8

It was Saturday afternoon with a light breeze outside, but still humid. Dominoe arrived at her cousin's house Liz, who lived in Marrero off Barataria Bay Blvd just twenty minutes from Dominoe. Liz was the punk rocker type girl with bright red hair, piercings on her eyebrow and ears, dark green checker shorts and converse shoes.

Dominoe knocked on the door waiting for an answer. "Hi long time, long see." Liz said with excitement as they hugged each other, walking to the living room to catch up after a year. Dominoe explained all what was going on and how she thinks others know about the happenings but are not saying anything. She even suggested that she was crazy for some reason and didn't want to admit it to herself. Liz placed her water down and grabbed Dominoes hand explaining. "I've seen and heard things in the haunted attraction part of the school, but never been in the active school part. There was a tragic unexpected death that happened while I worked at the haunted house. Larry was his name. Larry was an engineer that did the effects and props of the haunted house. He was driving home from a business trip to pick his family up for a vacation and was killed by a drunk driver. People have claimed to have seen him roaming the haunted house and have felt a tap by their shoulder, things being moved inside and a cold breeze. He was considered a joking, but friendly type of spirit, not a harmful one. Many believe he is the good spirit that roams the haunt just trying to make it known he is there and still has his sense of humor." She showed Dominoe a picture of him, he was five three with short spiky black hair and brown eyes, but she didn't recognize the man in the photograph. "Shaggy one of the volunteers had a Polaroid photo he took of himself in a mirror inside the haunted house, others claimed to see a body figure in the mirror that looked like Larry. Nobody has seen Shaggy in a long time, I till this day have never seen that photo and probably never will."

Dominoe sat there looking at Liz confused. "The noises I hear are of a little girl and the growl I heard was not friendly at all, it was quite evil." Liz paused placing her hand on her chin. "There had been stories of people hearing loud footsteps like of a drill sergeant and a voice of a man yelling, get out of here! There were stories of piles of bricks knocked down and a whole set that was not fully finished knocked down hard." "When you worked there did any of Y'all do something that could possibly bring negative energy into the place?" Liz took a deep breath and sat next to Dominoe. "The story I'm about to tell you stays between us and us only, understand?" "Yes." "There was an incident that could have brought something else to that place, something evil. A night I and others will never forget but want to."

Part 2

1988-1989

Chapter 9

It was the end of October. The air was clean with the scent of fall, the first year in the opening of the haunted attraction was a success. The school was almost shut down due to bankruptcy. The directors could not leave innocent children to nowhere learning to speak. The project was a two-month bloodshed, after getting all the asbestos out of the building, it was all constructed by a talented group of people that consisted of the names of Larry, Olga Liz, Edward, Emily, Eric, Louis and Dominic.

The actors and tour guides came along after word of mouth. The first night was a disaster and a poor show up about ten people with the lack of advertisement. As the nights went the more people came and by Halloween night the place was a gold mind to raise enough money to save the school. There was even a little left over to put on the side, for the next year of the haunted house. The directors and teachers voted to keep the attraction on going year after year with most money going to the school and the rest for the attraction. The haunted house was so popular there was already a list of volunteers waiting to join the next season and ready to come and help out on building and painting as soon as possible.

The haunted house part became a hangout for the teenagers that worked there. It was full of eighteen to twenty-one-year old's playing hide and go seek in the dark, or just sitting in the cast room getting drunk while watching horror movies all night on VHS. They were all let in by Eric, who had a key to the place, he was Mr. Edward's nephew. He was one of the construction workers who helped build all the walls that linger through the dark halls of the building. The group became friends and nicknamed themselves the NUGS, which stood for "new useless guys or girls." They didn't do much being new to this and sometimes were considered the constructor worker's bitches.

A meeting was scheduled a month after October in regards of what scenes will stay and what will go. There was also talk about doing an awards ceremony for the best of the best in the haunted house to show some appreciation to the dedicated volunteers working there for just a hot dog and one can drink a night. Merchandise was even sold half price after the season was over. The 1989 season was prepped and was set to begin construction in next March. There main designer and funny man

Larry was set to travel to a meeting for his job and had a vacation set with his family.

It was a dark rainy evening, Larry had no idea what he was in for. He was driving at the speed limit just talking to his wife on a pay phone. He told her he loved her and the usual, then began driving back on the road to get to his family and start their fun. When out of nowhere he got hit from the side by a drunk driver, flipping his car three times dying instantly. The news to his family and haunted house friends was shocking and heart breaking. He was a loving family man and a very hard worker, his passion for the haunted house had no words.

They found stuff he was working on in his shed for the next season along with papers and designs for effects after his death. The stuff he had in mind was given to Mr. Edward. They tried doing all what he had as a last request and a tribute to his legacy, but only some worked. Only Larry knew what he was doing and how to make his prop effects work.

The funeral was a large turn out with all friends and family, right after the funeral all volunteers went back to the haunted house to pay tribute to him, by releasing balloons all at once into the air and watching the wind blow it away and disappear forever. There was booze and music involved, they decided to go out with a bang for Larry, so he was not forgotten.

Chapter 10

It was almost New Year's and another successful year in the books for their haunted house. The NUGS were all talking about weird things happening inside the haunted house. They thought since it was a haunted house it was meant to be creepy.

One night they were all playing hide and go seek, Emily was hiding inside the wolf shack scene, she felt a wind of cold air hit her. She raised her hand in the air to feel where the cold was coming from, she then felt a tap on her shoulder. Emily ran out from the back of the haunted house into the cast room. Everyone stood there in silence till Dominic spoke up saying how he experience the same thing and it freaked him out. Freaked him out? Dominic was a six five muscular bald head male that did local body building competitions and looked like he could hurt someone, and he was freaked out? They all stood there for a while in silence like they were waiting for a calling or something to happen. Without hesitation they all walked out in their cars and left the place only to speak each other on the phone as the days went by.

Liz was good friends with Freddy, who began hanging out

and becoming a NUG. He studied the paranormal but knew a friend who was more advanced in it, who did investigations for free. He suggested bringing him for observation and maybe trying to do what he does. They all decided to meet back there on New Year's Eve with booze, to see what, this ghost person can do and find at their hangout.

Chapter 11

The days passed, it was finally New Year's Eve and the end of 1989. It was the start of a brand-new decade. The sky was dark and foggy from all the fireworks, the smell of gun powder drifting through the air. The temperature was in the high fifties, feeling like the early thirties, with no rain expected. The group got back together in the cast room, Freddy brought his friend Alton to investigate the school.

The group followed him around looking at him weird the whole time. "Did someone recently die here?" Alton asked. They told him about the death of Larry but did not die on location. Alton stopped looking into the air. "It appears he has not left this earth and that he does not want to leave this place for some reason. He is to attach to it to let go." The NUGS looked at each other, shrugging their shoulders confused. "He is the one doing the hauntings, unless this place is built on an Indian burial ground or there were actual deaths in here, then it can't be anyone else." There were deaths there, but not in the same building. Both buildings were connected to one another some way and could possibly spread the spirits around.

Alton walked around for about two hours getting nothing, it was now one hour till midnight and everyone was all boozed up. Alton was the biggest drunk, but not being an asshole or threatening anyone. He reached into his bag and pulled out something that none of the NUGS had ever seen before. A dark stained wood Ouija board. The NUGS heard nothing but bad things about a Ouija board. The room was silent, even with consumed alcohol the presence of this board was frightening.

Chapter 12

The NUGS placed their jaws up after being dropped when the Ouija board was brought out. They sat there silent, all Alton did was laugh and look at them with a creepy face. The group was not comfortable at all being in the same room with a Ouija board, but were all young and up to experiencing new things.

Alton took his right arm waving it for everybody to sit down. "Relax guys I've done this a hundred times it's not harmful I promise, it's just an unexplained game that you play to reach out to the spirits." Everyone sat down slowly putting their hands on their side as Alton set up the Ouija board. He began lighting candles before turning out the lights. Alton grabbed the planchette from the box, placing it on the board, placing both hands on it, moving it around. "I will now open the circle, so we can speak to whoever is here." He asked the first question. "Is there a spirit in here with us right now?" He kept his hand on the planchette waiting, within seconds it moved along with his hand spelling out, "yes." Alton grabbed it again asking out loud. "What is your name spirit?" The planchette moved again and everyone in the room gasped, holding their breath for a split second when it spelled out, "Larry." Liz was starting to freak out, this was not battery operated no one underneath the table, this truly was the devils game that was described by people. "I can't do this I want to go now." Liz replied panicking and breathing heavenly, Alton told her and everyone to relax when the door of the cast room flew open blowing out the candles and a loud growl coming from everyone's ear. The glass in the office broke like a baseball flying through from a play. Everyone got up running out of there screaming while leaving the Ouija board. They all stood around outside panicking and crying with disbelief of what just happened in there. Freddy tried to calm Liz down. "Great look what you did asshole! You scared her half to death!" "I... I I'm sorry. I never seen this happen before I swear," Alton stuttered. "Well you started this shit now you're going to finish it. You go back in there and you destroy that demonic piece of shit!" "Ok I'll go back in and get rid of it everyone just stay here and remain calm."

Calm was not happening anytime soon for the NUGS, as Alton went back inside. He turned on the lights, after what he just experienced he did not want anything to do with the Ouija board ever again. He grabbed some of the rum he spotted on the sofa pouring it on the Ouija board and pulled out his zippo lighter. He watched what he used number of times burn right before his eyes, he can hear a loud band of whispers coming from the room like it was souls asking for help from him. He walked out the room telling the NUGS. "It's done, I burned it now it's just a pile of ashes."

Freddy tied his long wavy brown hair into a pony tail as he entered back into the cast room. He gathered all the ashes and threw it away. The NUGS cleaned their party mess and did not celebrate no more pass midnight. They locked the door, swearing that they would never speak of this incident and will never do this ever again in this building. Little did they know burning a Ouija board can bring a curse to the family or place where they did this act? The right way to get rid of a Ouija board is to break it into seven pieces, sprinkle it with holy water and bury it far away from the location, like deep in the woods. The building and the group were now cursed from the board, with no turning back. The spirits weren't all friendly after that night. An eviler presence escaped into the halls of the buildings. There were ways to cleanse away their souls, but nobody to step up and make it happened, instead they ignored the reality and made it imagination.

Part 3

1995

Chapter 13

Dominoe was in shock after hearing this story. The lady that died on the steps was not just a force by spirits, it was caused by a drunkenness, childless past. Dominoe was in rage at her cousin and friends for doing that, bringing a curse to the school and to themselves. "The school was already cursed Dominoe, before we stepped foot in it. We just extended the curse with welcome arms from a Satanic toy." Liz got up from her seat bursting into tears, she explained how she had been watching herself and hoping the curse does not bring anything bad upon her.

Alton apparently was claimed to have gotten heavier into drugs and alcohol and was not heard from for weeks till they went into his apartment and found him in his bathtub dead with both wrists sliced from the broken glass of a picture frame of his mother. The others are either in bad shape of health or dead. "The drill sergeant people hear could have been from the door we opened that night, some think that he is the evil bastard who caused the massacre of 1970 at the school," Liz said calmly.

"What is this dark history everyone keeps talking about? Why no one will say anything?!" Dominoe demanded. "Because no one likes talking about it and now that I and friends are cursed, we definitely try to forget about it. If you truly want to know what happened look it up, if you are still not convinced and want to know if there is anything more going on there, hire a medium to get some answers." Dominoe sat down putting her hand over her face in disbelief that her cousin was involved with something like this. "Ouija boards and seances can bring anything negative to the area, it's not recommended if you do not know what you are doing which in Y'all cases did not know nothing." Liz looked at her in disbelief. "I have sort of been researching this stuff." "How you think I feel Dominoe, I didn't want to do it, but was a part of it anyway. If I can go back I would not be there, I would be at home away from that cursed night that marked us all."

They finished their drink. Liz talked about after that night she gave up on the haunted house eventually because she was getting old for it and had a life outside of it to take care of. She admitted to hearing things early hours of the morning, but just turned to the other side ignoring it. She admitted to something following her home that was attached to her.

Liz hired a voodoo queen to come and bless her house two years ago. She usually lights certain candles to keep away negative energy, she's had bad luck with boys and goes through job to job. She believed all of this, along with her parents not talking to her to be a cause of this curse brought upon them from that night. She regretted what they did that night and for even knowing Freddy to bring his friend Alton doing that. Liz reminded Dominoe of the ghost stories that she encountered there and what people said, no doubt something lurks those school halls, but no one has dared to see who or what. Anyone who does encounter something nowadays keeps it to themselves. "My advice right now Dominoe is research the history to get an idea of what you are dealing with at your job. Look into the past and if you truly don't believe what you are hearing and feeling, hire a medium. It is the only way to have closure." Dominoe grabbed her purse and gave her cousin a hug thanking her for all the advice. She drove back home in tears and in fear that Liz and her friends are doomed for their future. She thought about hiring a seance session of people who knew what they were doing, but after hearing about that eerie New Year's Eve story, she felt there was enough doors open.

Chapter 14

Dominoe tossed and turned all night, having the worst nightmare ever. She dreamed of being in a dark room alone with just a Ouija board. She asked the board if she was alone, it replied no. She then asked who was with her and it replied death. A black hand with sharp yellow nails popped out the board, dragging her in it.

She awoke right when she was about to be sucked into the board. Her skin was sweaty her breathing was heavy. She fell back asleep for two more hours than awoke on a bright Sunday morning, the day before the next day of school. Dominoe had no appetite, but her body was begging for coffee to stay awake. She was hesitant to research being afraid of what she might find. She knew no one would approve of this medium at the school, it would have to be done on a non-school day. She also knew no one would come out about their own experiences there. She was alone in this task and had a choice to make.

The next day came, it started out not so bad or eerie. She began doing paper work holding her Mickey Mouse silver pin she got back in her last year of college. She was writing with a clear mind when all sudden she got a fragrance smell in the air of perfume. She sniffed trying to follow where it was coming from. Then in a split second the fragrance disappeared from the air and all she can smell is the cleanness of the building. She believed that someone was there trying to get her attention but did not know who. She had enough with the questions, it was time for her to go home and finally research this so called dark history she is getting fed up hearing about.

The school day was done and Dominoe was in a hurry to get away and go home. She did five miles over the speed limit making it home an extra ten minutes earlier. She walked in, taking a quick ten-minute shower while her coffee brewed. She got out the shower, fixed her a cup of coffee and sat by the computer in her puppy paw pajamas. She was ready to get any information she can about Hope Institute Aka Bloodstone Institute. She felt the world just stood still for a moment she can hear water dripping from the sink, the grandfather clock ticking and the walls making a cracking sound. She took a sip of her coffee, a deep breath and searched to see what exactly happened at the school.

Part 4

1962-1970

Chapter 15

The year was 1962. The world was going through the peace phase and the Vietnam War. The school was taken charge by Sister Elizabeth Foret. Elizabeth was a quiet woman, an honor student in school, never in trouble or abused, just lonely with her beauty features. She got involved with alcohol in her early twenties, drowning her depression into a bottle every night. Both her parents were dead from a fire, no siblings, hardly any family left to go to for support. Elizabeth was driving on a rainy night, crashing into a tree and almost dying on side of the road. She wished she would have died being so miserable and lonely, but at the same time was blessed to be alive from that crash. She walked into a church a day after being released from the hospital, staring at the lit candles on her knees, praying to God. That was when she found God and an opportunity for a second chance in life. She decided to become a nun devoting her soul to the catholic religion.

The Vietnam War started in 1955, leaving the United States in a peace war against the real war. Elizabeth was doing her partying on the streets of New Orleans at the start of the war, few years later she was a walking servant of God. The aftermath of the crash and now a nun, she still felt like something was missing in her life. A family of her own. She couldn't get married or have kids now being a devoted nun, it was against her religion. She walked out the church bursting into tears, getting that empty feeling on the inside once again.

One rainy night she decided to go to a bar on 4th street in Marrero, ordering a water to drink to test her alcoholism. This time era was white's vs black's, the segregation era. It was a very hard time in the U.S., but Elizabeth ignored it. She accepted everyone as equal and felt it wasn't right to choose a color like a Civil War. She sat down drinking her water being stared at like she was scum. She looked down realizing she was in her nun uniform. She removed her veil exposing her beautiful brunette hair but got no man's attention. She was about to leave when a tall slim black man in an Army uniform came in. Her eyes were locked on him as he smiled waving his hat to her. He went to the bar for a drink, the bartender refused to serve him cause of his skin color and asked him to leave. The man walked out peacefully, Elizabeth left her water and ran out the door stopping the gentlemen. "Excuse me, sir? I am so sorry about that, you are a military man and do not deserve such treatment. You fight for our country I respect you so much." "Thank you mam that is so kind of you. My name is Major Jonathan T. Coleman and you are?" He said raising his hand out. "Elizabeth, Sister Elizabeth."

 They both shook hands and left the bar to go back to his small house off Avenue A. He put on an Elvis record, his favorite artist as they both sipped on scotch while sitting on the sofa getting to know each other. Elizabeth kept staring at his little gray spot on top of his hair, he was in his thirties and already starting to gray.

They talked for hours laughing and smiling with the music playing in the background. After a few drinks they went into the bedroom, where they made love until the rain stopped. They laid there quietly staring at the ceiling until they fell asleep with the rain starting again.

 They awoke the next morning, Jonathan was shocked and scared for sleeping with a nun. He was in fear of ruining her and in fear of what would happen to him. She grabbed his hand as he was hurrying to dress. "My beliefs are still here, but my thoughts on marriage and intercourse have been a dream of mine for a while now. I have a hole in my heart Jonathan and it's making me fade fast." Jonathan placed his right arm over the side of her face kissing her. "I have a hole in my heart too, and it's about to burn because I am getting shipped off to Vietnam in two days. We should get married that way I have something worth fighting for to come back to and you have something worth living for." Elizabeth shed tears in happiness and agreed to get married. "We must keep this a secret either way Jonathan, or we will be crucified for sure. Only problem is, who were going to find to do this?" "I know someone who will help," Jonathan replied holding her in silence for a while. They felt their hole being covered inside. They talked some more, Elizabeth mentioned having a child was a piece missing too. They decided that when the time was right for a child she would quit so she can have a regular birth and be able to raise her own child. They went to a justice of the peace, Jonathan paid off the judge to keep shut about their marriage. He knew the judge growing up, it was the only way for them to be legally married. Jonathan promised after he kissed the bride that one day when the war was over he would give her the wedding she always dreamed of. They celebrated their last night before deployment with a romantic dinner filled with music and passionate love. They thought of trying for a baby that night just in case something happens, but Jonathan felt leaving a mother alone to raise a child and with the circumstances was a selfish act to do.

It was the day of his deployment, they both held each other crying in the living room, hoping to see each other again. Elizabeth gave Jonathan a picture of herself for him to keep and stare at when he got lonely or scared. Jonathan walked out the door waving. He let her stay there as long he was gone, to keep up with the bills and the house. Jonathan was going to oversee his own platoon cause of his ranking. He never feared anything even being chased by men in white sheets, but for the first time he was fearing for his life. With his new wife he now had something to fight for and come back home to finish his life with. He planned on writing her every chance he got, he was not going to forget why he was there fighting for his country, regardless on some of it not being on his side. They both knew nothing of each other really but felt like they knew each other forever. It was one of those loves at first sight, meant to be together forever.

Chapter 16

It was a week after Jonathan's deployment, Elizabeth was as happy as she had ever been. She started to feel her hole get sealed with happiness. He wrote to her as much as he could, explaining the green fields, the mud walks, the explosions, fire and people coming from the ground. The sound of the cries of children and men that he slept with in his nightmares, but the visual image of her face when he closed his eyes. Elizabeth dropped tears on his letters, happy to be called his wife, but feared him being over there. She stared at the kids out the window a lot, watching them laugh and smile. Her priority now was tending to the school, then tend to the house. She kept a photo of Jonathan in her pocket that she grabbed from his piano staring at it randomly throughout the day.

On a bright morning, Elizabeth wrote a letter back to Jonathan, to mail it off secretly. She was introduced to the new nun to look after some of the children. Her name was Pam O' Flynn from Ireland, her pretty blue eyes brightened the room. Her red hair was covered by her nun veil, the beauty that really brought her out. She came to America when she was an infant.

Her parents were looking for more opportunities and heard of this place called America. Pam learned sign language at a young age, that's when she wanted to help teach deaf children to speak better. Her biggest inspiration was her deaf sister; Pam would spend a few hours a day teaching her as much as possible. Her sister now rests in the New Orleans Cemetery. She was running into the street to get her kite, not hearing the delivery truck coming and was hit, dying instantly. Pam vowed to help children any which way she could for the rest of her life, especially since learning to teach children to speak has progressed since her time as a child. Sister Elizabeth welcomed Pam with open arms, showing her around the school. Hope Institute was a lovely sight at this time, the sun shining over it would make it look like heaven was standing on it. Sister Elizabeth showed her to the classroom, walking back to her office to stare at Jonathan's photo again.

 Two years passed, Jonathan was still in the war writing to Elizabeth, she was writing back. She felt like she was never going to have a life outside the school and time was running out. She had to have faith and be patient with the life she really wanted. The patience of waiting would take a toll to Elizabeth, a turning point in her life that would affect others as well.

Chapter 17

It was 1964, the war was still going on; more lives being lost in the muddy hell over there. Elizabeth has not received a letter from Jonathan in months, in fear he was killed over there, no one knew of their marriage so getting to her was impossible. She usually wrote back to him when he wrote her, but for once she wrote to him first. It wasn't a long letter to him, but just enough to try and reach out to him hoping that he was alive.

Weeks passed and still no letters from Jonathan, she began to drink a glass of scotch every night. Her sober years were now ruined for being impatient on waiting for an answer from her secret husband. She would look at herself in the mirror, seeing another side of herself, almost like a demon coming out of her body. She had waited long enough and presumed the love of her life was dead. The sister that was once loved, feeding kind around the school began to grow to an attitude, arrogant presence to the nuns. The very polite Irish nun Pam was so sweet to Sister Elizabeth, but whatever she told Sister Elizabeth was back fired into her. The thought of her lost husband hasn't only reopened the hole in her heart, but also opened a new personality that grew stronger and more dangerous as the days went by.

The whole school noticed the change in Sister Elizabeth. They wrote letters, made phone calls trying to get her out. When Sister Elizabeth found out about this, she threatened the whole school if they ever tried it again. No one was safe there and no one was happy being a part of that place. An evil presence was growing like a cancer into the heart of the school, Sister Elizabeth was capable of having things her way.

Pam was teaching the students like she promised, she was quite attached to one little girl named Susan. She was the most adorable little deaf child in the world, especially when her brown pig tails moved in the air when she jumped around. Pam would sit at the desk coloring with Susan every day, Susan would draw for Pam. Pam placed some of the photos on her wall where she admired Susan's art. Sister Elizabeth would rip the pictures in pieces in front of Pam, being disrespectful to that innocent child. Pam cried watching the pieces fall to the ground, as she gathered them off the floor quickly before Susan would come in. After a while Pam began hiding Susan's art and would bring it home to place on her refrigerator.

Sister Elizabeth got so cruel, she began to sign language to the children that there was no God and no guarantee that they will ever learn to speak. She would say it with an evil smile and walk out the room like she did no wrong. There was a bet going around about who would push Sister Elizabeth down the stairs to save the day. It was an inside joke really but was tempted to all the nuns wanting to see her gone.

It was a dark, rainy afternoon the school was quiet, dark on the inside with lights flickering on and off. Sister Elizabeth was in her office drinking warm tea, she pulled out the photo of Jonathan staring at it with tears. "What have I become? She sobbed. "You made me do this you son of a bitch." Her office door opened hard, slamming against the wall with an echo. Sister Elizabeth stood up in shock, staring at Jonathan, who was staring at her back dripping wet. He had an evil mean look with a scar going across his face. "Jonathan…. you're alive. I thought you were dead?" "Gee, no honey I'm glad to see you, just your alive and shocked?" He muttered walking up to her, grabbing her hand tightly in pain. "Ouch Jonathan your hurting me." "What's wrong, you don't want anyone to know about us bitch?!" She cried, begging him to let her go, he then slammed her against the wall. "You get home now, no excuses!" He yelled, exiting the room fast. She laid on the ground crying, this was not the same man she married before he left. What did Vietnam do to him? She thought to herself, feeling a knot on her head from being slammed. All the letters, the waiting, he was back like she wanted, but now after what he did to her, she wished he was dead.

Chapter 18

School wasn't over, but she felt the need to do what her husband said before something worse happened. She exits out the school, running in the pouring rain, no one knew what happened in the office. No one knew what was going on with Sister Elizabeth's secret life that had been hidden these years. She drove fast in the rain, driving through red lights, hopping to crash and die before getting home.

She arrived home, Jonathan was inside sitting at the kitchen table waiting for his dinner. She began to cook, trying to hurry before her husband loses it, dropping and splattering things while rushing. Jonathan threw his boot at her with impatient force. Cursing at her with every word in the dictionary.

She placed his dinner on the table, he took a sniff and bite. "How is it?" Jonathan looked up at her with a grin spitting it out throwing his plate off the table and punching her in the gut. "This taste like shit! You mean to tell me all this time alone, you didn't learn to cook good once?" He grabbed her by the hair. "Now pick this mess up and fix me something better and eatable." She cried on the floor while picking up the broken plate and food, he was out of control.

She kept noticing the scar on his face that wasn't there before he left. She assumed he got shot or hit by something during the war and had brain damage from the wound. It was the only explanation of his behavior, or he could have been shell shocked from the war. She would try to question the war, but he would just beat her or scream in rage.

Sister Elizabeth went through three tough years of abuse from Jonathan. He would rape her then she would miscarriage from being thrown down. After so many miscarriages, the dream of having a little family was now long gone. She couldn't get pregnant no matter how many times he raped her. No one knew of the happenings outside the school, but her patients grew thinner inside the school. Her anger from home was brought to work as a vent of power in leading the school, to get the heat off her shoulders. She tried suicide again and again but would always get caught in the act and was given far much worse punishment from Jonathan for trying it. She began to not feel the pain; she was so used to it that it didn't appeal to her body. She felt that she will die with whatever plan God or whoever had in stored for her. She began questioning her religion far long time ago, but all the abuse she questioned beyond that. Her husband once slapped her across the face, knocking her off the hospital bed threatening her that he would kill her next time. She did what he was told no matter how bad it was and just lived life the best she can take everything out on her nuns at work.

Chapter 19

It was 1967 nothing changed at school or outside of it. Sister Pam became close to another student. A little blonde-haired girl named Kelly. She began coughing loudly as the year went by, her parents had no money to bring her to the doctor. Pam brought the coughing to the attention to the other sisters, they wanted to put in money to bring this child to a doctor, but Sister Elizabeth thought otherwise. Pam for the first time brought out her rage building from the inside toward Sister Elizabeth. "You witch!" Sister Elizabeth turned around in shock. "What did you just call me?" "You're a witch, an evil witch, you have no care for these children or the school. You shouldn't even be the one running this school!" Sister Elizabeth slapped Sister Pam across the face, knocking her to the ground. She looked up at Sister Elizabeth holding the side of her face in tears. "You picked the wrong time to grow some guts against me. Now I am in charge and what I say goes. That little girl will be fine, let Mother Nature run its course to get that cold out of her body. You ever talk to me like that again sister, I will throw you out my window and watch you bleed to death." Sister Pam got up running out the room and out the school in a panic. Sister

Elizabeth became her husband in female form, no one even would look at her while walking by anymore.

On a foggy morning Kelly was playing with her bouncing ball and coughing louder than ever, gasping for air. Sister Pam went to get some water for Kelly, when she came back, she saw her lying on the floor with her pretty blue eyes wide open not breathing. She tried performing CPR on her but could not bring her back to life. The coroner came to pick up her body, autopsy showed she died of Pneumonia and was not treated in time to be saved. Sister Pam was devastated by the death of this poor innocent child and was drifting from the atmosphere of the school, with the continuing of Sister Elizabeth's behavior the school was going down a hole.

Sister Pam was spotted by people on her knees, thinking she was praying, but she was talking to herself. The sisters began to think Sister Pam was going mad from Kelly's death and because of the school. Sister Elizabeth approached her one morning with a grin on her face. "Everyone looks at you like you've lost your mind Sister Pam, you're making a fool of yourself and embarrassing the future of our organization. After this school year is over your gone, I can't risk having crazies teaching my students." She walked away with no soul and no expression, just that stupid grin she gave everyone. All the nuns were staring at Pam some giggled at her, she ran back inside the school crying and never feeling so embarrassed in her life. She sat in the corner crying seeing an apparition form of Kelly hugging her telling her it will be alright. The suspicious of Sister Pam talking to herself was that she was talking to the ghost of little Kelly.

It was a sunny afternoon March 18th, Sister Pam was quiet then usual and barely taught the students anything all morning. Sister Elizabeth thought she was up to something and asked the others to keep an eye on her.

It was recess Sister Pam was nowhere to be found, Sister Elizabeth was in hopes she quit and left so she would not have to deal with her no more. Out in the courtyard, everyone can hear a voice that sounded like Sister Pam from the distance. "Up here everyone!" Everyone outside raised their heads up in shock, Sister Pam was at the top of the ledge of the school. "You all think I'm crazy, I am not the crazy one, she is the crazy one!" She shouted, pointing at Sister Elizabeth. Everyone stared at Sister Elizabeth as she gave an evil look at everyone as they turned their heads back to Sister Pam. "I have been talking to little Kelly's spirit, she can talk and hear now. She is OK now and in peace! Kelly I am so sorry; this is for you!" Sister Pam jumped off the ledge landing face first on the concrete ground of the courtyard. The blood puddle spreaded all over the concrete staining it red. All the nuns circled the body sobbing away, but Sister Elizabeth walked away smiling. She walked right back into the school as the ambulance sirens got closer to the school sitting at her desk, pulling out a small glass of scotch to pour into her glass. She raised her glass up. "A toast to you Sister Pam, for putting a smile on my face. Something I haven't done in a long time, cheers to you crazy."

Chapter 20

After the suicide incident the school fell apart, parents pulled students out from them being traumatize watching Sister Pam fall off the roof. They didn't feel safe leaving their children to people they didn't trust no more. The sisters tried so many times the past two years to get rid of Sister Elizabeth, no one cared or believed them, there was a rumor that Sister Elizabeth broke one of the sister's arm. Her arrogance was unalterable, sisters quit the school, requested for transfers, anything to get away from that hell. Sister Elizabeth continued the fight at home being abused and rape, it was part of her life now, and she felt numb from all of it.

It was a cold December in 1970, the record player was playing Christmas songs throughout the school speakers. Sister Elizabeth was sipping on hot cocoa, after fighting all these years the Archdiocese finally sent a letter to Sister Elizabeth that stated she would be fired or forced to retire early for her actions at the school. She felt her life was officially going through hell in a hand basket. She began a year earlier poisoning Jonathan's food little by little. She wanted him to die slowly on the inside like she has been all these years. He began to cough more every day, he was too stubborn and stupid to go to a doctor. She became his nurse at home and had no idea what she would do with her life after this chapter was closed from marriage to no more school. She had money saved, thought of moving across seas, no one would know or care if she died. Nobody she cared for was left in the world, dying alone was a mission stamped to her soul.

The children were learning in their classrooms as the music played on the speaker. The students couldn't hear the music but felt the vibration in their ears from it. The sisters were humming to the tunes; it had been the first nice thing Sister Elizabeth did while being a hateful witch.

The wind was heavy outside, sounded like a roaring lion beating against the window. The hallway was silent, until the front doors slammed open so hard it shattered the glass from the windows. Jonathan entered the school wearing his dark Army green jacket and black pants. He had his pistol in his right hand, yelling in rage while coughing his lungs up. "Elizabeth!" Everybody in the school stopped and panic from the sound of his voice. The children were worried looking up at the Sisters faces of fear.

He began firing at the statues and windows, the children could not hear, but felt the vibration of the ricochet of the gun. The sisters began trying to hide the students or escaped the school. He walked up the steps entering a classroom of ten students raising his pistol at them as they started to cry. He opened fire at the sister and ten children killing them all. He reloaded his gun, shooting sisters as they ran through the hall, students ran in the corners frighten for their lives. He shot anyone in sight, leaving no survivors and no expression on his face. At the end of the hall, sitting in her desk calm with her grin was Elizabeth waiting for Jonathan to walk in. It was a show down waiting to happen, two soulless bodies about settle this matter once for all.

Chapter 21

The classrooms and hallways were stained with puddles of blood from the shots. Sisters and students laid in the puddles still and cold with eyes wide open. Jonathan coughed until his face turned red while walking slowly to Sister Elizabeth. Their eyes locked each other, Sister Elizabeth showed no sign of fear. He pulled out a bottle of poison from his pocket, slamming it on top of her desk. "You mind explaining this bitch?" She picked it up, staring at it. "I'm sorry you don't like my secret recipes?" He began to cough some more this time coughing blood into the palm of his hand. He stared at his hand wiping the blood on his jacket staring back at her laughing. "Oh, you're going to get it now bitch."

He raised his gun at her. "Now I am going to do what you tried doing to yourself so many times. I am going to put you out of your misery since you want me out of mine." "Wait!" She replied fast raising her hands up, walking slowly to him. "You once completed my heart when you were the man I loved. I know that man is still inside he's just lost and can't ever be found again, all I want is one more kiss."

They both stared at each other in silence for a few minutes,

Jonathan began to cry, something he had not done since that night he left her for Vietnam. He placed the gun down placing his hands into her face, giving her a kiss. The kiss felt just like the ones he gave years ago. Elizabeth began to cry as they kissed while grabbing a pair of long, sharp pointy scissors, stabbing him in the side of his throat. His voice began to squeal and choke, the blood running down the side of his neck like a faucet. He raised the gun to her forehead as he was bleeding to death. Sister Elizabeth stood still closing her eyes as he opened fire hitting her right between the eyes.

He walked weakly down the hallway, falling down the stairs, crawling his way into the next building where he rested in a classroom near the window till the last drop of blood spilled out. His body was left there stiff with his eyes wide open and a smile on his face for the first time in years. The nightmare was over between the fight at home and at school.

Chapter 22

Only the victims that day, heard the shots of the school. One of the surviving sisters, Angela called 911. She was barely alive when she called, but dead once the police showed. The cops arrived five minutes after the call was made opening the door with their guns pointed in the air. They saw the trail of blood Jonathan left that entered to the next building. Two cops went to check on that trail while the rest went upstairs.

When they got to the first classroom the site was something they have never seen before. Poor innocent children and nuns lying in a puddle of their own blood. The nuns had rosaries in their hand covered in blood splatters, the sight of blood was unbearable. Cops said the color of the blood stains was like the blood-stones on a heliotrope rock giving the school the nickname, Bloodstone Institute.

The news and papers talked about the massacre for months, but the memory never ended. The school fell for decades after the massacre, parents had no other choice then to bring their children to the school because it was the only one that existed in the area. Parents began a petition for funding another school for the deaf, in time it fell through. The dark history still gets talked about, but doesn't like being spread or brought up, most people keep it hush like it never happened, and all anybody could do is go on with the history and try not to repeat itself.

They went away with nuns teaching the school in due time as a change of scenery. The change wasn't much though, as the rumors and past still came back to haunt the school. They found young adults with college degrees to run the school, keeping it religious. The school is still running by religion politics not listening to the parents on the outside, as long money was coming in they will keep the school going, or at least till they are bored with it.

Part 5

1995

Chapter 23

Dominoe stayed up all night reading stories and articles on the history of the murders in 1970. She got nauseous from the picture that she saw and of the story itself. It was one of those rare photos from the case file that the public never got to see. The blood, the innocent souls laying there. Nobody knew of this black man, Jonathan, police closed the case of the man being shell shock and lost it. Why take it out on this school of all places? If the school was haunted, it's because of this massacre and Liz's New Year's incident. The negative energy could be this Jonathan guy, or something else brought through the doorway that her cousin and group of friends opened from the Ouija board.

It was five in the morning, Dominoe still had a cup of coffee by her side. She had to be up in just a few hours for school. Sleep was the last thing on her mind after reading all the gruesome facts from Hope Institutes past. She watched the sunrise while sipping on coffee, taking a deep breath not wanting to get up. She had lost her appetite after seeing that disturbing photo on the internet. She got dressed with a stomach full of caffeine. She thought about those pour children and nuns, she started to hear random crying screams in her mind. She was also amazed by Sister Elizabeth's long history of behavior. Why did this woman stay in charge so long and be so hateful? Thinking to herself.

Dominoe arrived at school, yawning as she exited her car. She was now starting to feel the lack of sleep from staying up all night. She greeted everyone good morning, Ms. Maria knocked at her door. "Hi Dominoe, I'm not going to keep you, I just wanted to tell you that you're doing a great job." Dominoe looked up with her pretty big brown eyes smiling. "Thank you, Ms. Maria that means a lot." Ms. Maria left the office, Dominoe just smiled. The school was scaring her mentally, but she felt accomplished hearing that from upper management. She sat at her desk all day going in and out of sleep sitting up while doing paperwork. She turned on her coffee machine in her corner to wake up some more, rubbing her eyes, then staring at the doorway. A little blonde-haired girl stood by the door staring at her. She had never seen this girl before. The little girl was very cute in her red and white polka dot dress. The little girl reached her hand out for Dominoe to take it. "Follow me." The little girl said shy fully. Dominoe rubbed her eyes again seeing this little girl asking her to come with her. She didn't know if she was in a dream or reality. The little girl walked away as Dominoe followed, leading her into a classroom that was full of blood, dead students and nuns. Dominoe panicked staring at the blood everywhere, in the middle of the classroom was a tall black man in a military jacket writing on the chalk board in blood that read "die, die, die." The black man turned around to face her with a pair of scissors in his neck and blood spilling out of the wound like a waterfall pouring on the floor. It was Jonathan the guy she saw pictures of from the internet. He raised a gun to her pulling the trigger, Dominoe closed her eyes screaming while falling. She opened them seeing the classroom back to normal and no bullet hole in her. The only sound she heard was of the children playing outside. She began sweating, inhaling and exhaling fast, walking slowly back to her office smelling the coffee brewed. She picked her coffee up to pour her some, but placed it back sitting back at the desk.

  School had let out, Dominoe packed her bags walking out

of the class fast. She stopped by the stairs, hearing a cry from the distance, hesitant going back after what she saw earlier, but turned right back around walking towards the cry. She walked into her office seeing a lady crying with her head planted on her desk. "Excuse me mam are you alright?" "He's coming to get me," she replied. "Who's is coming to get you?" "He's coming for me and everybody else." "Who mam?" The crying lady raised her head up with a bleeding bullet hole in her forehead. "Jonathan, he's here and he's coming for us all." Dominoe cried, running out of the building hearing the words "he's coming for us all" repeated and echoed all over.

    Dominoe sat in her car crying for ten minutes, feeling her heart race a million miles away. She turned the key and drove home, the only place she felt safe. She arrived home, taking her shoes off and placing her bag on the sofa. She laid on the sofa covering her face with a pillow, startled by the phone ringing. "Hello?" "Hi Dominoe, its Liz." She can hear Liz crying on the other end of the phone. "Liz what's wrong, it sounds like your crying?" "I am crying Dominoe, I have something to tell you." Dominoe closed her eyes taking a gulp in her mouth, not prepared what she was about to hear. "Are you sitting down Dominoe?" "Yes Liz." "I have been going to the doctor for two months now, I went today and well brace yourself. I have stage four colon cancer." Dominoe felt like the Earth stood still hearing the news. Dominoe was breathless and speechless on the phone all she can do was cry. "I'm coming over Liz." She hung up the phone, grabbed her keys and wallet racing to her cousin's house.

Chapter 24

Dominoes vision was becoming blurry from all the crying while driving to Liz's house. Baring to think of living in this world without her close cousin, she was too young for death with the future ahead of her. Dominoe arrived at her cousin's house wiping her eyes and cheeks after ringing the doorbell. "It's open!" Liz shouted softly.

Dominoe entered the house, seeing Liz sitting at the corner window smoking a cigarette. Liz wasn't crying just quiet and pale in the face. They hugged each other for a while without saying a word. Liz got her a bottle of water sitting back down taking tiny swallows. "I have been losing weight for a while unexpectedly, I thought it was just from me working too hard. Then I started shitting blood, that's when I got a concern. So, I went to the doctor after so many tests, today is when I got the worst news in the world. It's too late for chemotherapy, only giving me five months to live." Dominoe could not stop shedding tears, she was silent looking at her cousin, feeling bad for her. "I guess it finally happened, my curse finally burdened me." "No don't think that, it can't be!" Liz placed her arm on Dominoes left cheek rubbing her tear away. "You still don't believe in everything you see?" "Actually, after the day I had, I'm starting to second guess it." "Get a medium Dominoe, it is the only way you can bring closure and see what there is to believe. If that doesn't give you closure, then I don't know what will." "Let's not talk about that place Liz, let's just be together." Liz smiled at Dominoe. "OK." It took hours for Dominoe to calm down, all they can talk about was all the good times they had as kids. It was nine at night, Dominoe got up to go back home. "So, what are you going to do about the school?" Dominoe turned around taking a deep breath. "I'll hire a medium, your right it's the only way." They both hugged each other again, Liz did not show fear in her eyes Dominoe showed more fear then anything. Liz waved goodbye to Dominoe as she watched her leave.

Dominoe arrived back home, beginning to research local mediums. She wanted Stephanie Aerial, but she had just moved away to Florida, Dominoe couldn't ask someone to come a long way for this, she needed someone local and as soon as possible. She found a brother and sister team with highly reviews. Krystal and Dale Hebert, Krystal was pronounced dead three times on the table, but revived. Her brother Dale was fascinated by the dead and undead, works as her assistant on cases. They seemed promising to Dominoe, she dotted their phone number down to call and set a date. She also needed to figure out how to get them to the school without anyone knowing about it. There was a lot on her mind for bed, lack of sleep was coming from this long nightmare.

Dominoe awoke around two in the morning from a nightmare of a man strangling her repeating, "you can't save her." As she awoke and stared at the foot of her bed, she saw a shadow figure disappear into the hallway. There was no idea of what was witnessed, instead of getting up to inspect. She placed her head back down, closing her eyes forgetting what just happened. Two minutes later, three knocks came from the entrance to her bedroom. The mocking of the Act of Contrition, a demonic spirit had followed her home from the school. She raised up from her bed, grabbing the crucifix, reciting prayers all over the house. She was about to go back to bed when she heard glass break from the kitchen. She ran to the kitchen, finding glass cups and plates all over the floor and brownish blood coming from the faucet. She closed her eyes while pulling her hair, screaming in rage. "Leave my house now! Be gone you demonic creatures!" She opened her eyes, seeing the faucet stopped, just leaving a small puddle stain of the blood. The broken glass was everywhere, instead of jumping on the mess, she returned to her room, crying herself to sleep.

Chapter 25

It was a late cloudy Saturday off day at the end of September. It was just a week before the opening of the haunted house, Dominoe had not told anyone of her plan for that day. Dominoe had set up a schedule for the medium brother and sister to show up at around four. She wanted to get permission and keep it secret at the same time for what she was about to do.

She walked to the haunted house, bumping into a mid-fifties lady with short blondish white hair. "Can I help you sweetie?" She said with a smile. "Hi, I'm Dominoe the Executive Director of the school." They both reached out to shake hands. "Nice to finally meet you Dominoe, I'm Candie Reeve, the casting director for the haunted house." Dominoe heard of Ms. Candie, the lady who brought her son to the school to learn, then became a volunteer herself. Dominoe knew of her having keys to both buildings of the school, a very trustworthy lady. Dominoe took a gulp going straight to the point. "Ms. Candie how long have you volunteered here?" Candie looked up in the sky thinking. "Oh, I would say about four years." "In your four years here, have you experienced anything out of the ordinary?" "You mean like ghosts?" "Yes, like ghost?" Ms. Candie sat down slowly, hesitant to reply on the subject. "There are stories that float around, kids seeing full shape forms of people staring at them. Something passing fast in the exit hallways, loud sounds and cold chills coming from certain areas." "Do you have a story of your own?" Dominoe replied. Ms. Candie took a deep breath.

"I was in a scene by myself, they had a big pile of cinder blocks on the side. I was listening to the radio while painting, then out of nowhere the blocks all fell over. I freaked out and ran out of the room into the cast room, the scariest part was the way those blocks could have fallen is if an earthquake happened, or someone or something pushed them." Dominoes heart was racing hearing of the dangerous, scary story like that. "Ms. Candie, I have experienced a lot of weird things since I started last month, I need closure which is why I have a medium about to arrive any minute. I was wondering if you and the other volunteers can keep this a secret from the school and anyone else." Ms. Candie smiled at Dominoe grabbing her hand. "Under one condition, I get to stay and watch?" Dominoe smiled back and nodded. "The more people the more comfortable I'll feel, deal." They both shook hands and walked to the front waiting for the arrival of the medium.

It was after four, they both saw a short long blonde-haired lady and a bald head tall man walking towards them. "That must be them," Dominoe said, walking up to them. "Hi, I'm Krystal Hebert this is my brother Dale Hebert, were here for the investigation," she said in a country accent. They all shook hands and started walking to the building. Krystal stopped to stare at the same window Dominoe once stared at. "Everything OK?" "No, a nun died right here, she jumped off the roof and landed right there. I can feel her pain, all she wanted to do was help children and save this one who was very sick. We better start at the active school first."

Dominoe read the history of the school and the massacre again before bed last night to be familiar with anything just in case a clue or something came up. "Tell us a little about you Krystal." "Well I've talked to spirits since I was five, I was scared for a while, but then got used to it and knew how to control it. I knew it was a gift and didn't want it taken for granted." All lights in both buildings were taken off, Krystal pulled out a small candle lighting it. "Now I need everyone to remain silent and follow me closely." They walked on the top floor where Dominoes office and other classrooms were, calling for anyone or anything. Krystal's eyes widen looking in the classrooms. "Oh my, the blood, the pour souls. We must leave; this is too much to see." Ms. Candie and Dominoe saw nothing but knew of the massacre stories and did not want to see what Krystal was seeing.

Krystal stopped downstairs and opened her eyes looking at everyone. "I hear a distant voice of a woman; she is calling us to go to the other building." Dominoe took a gulp swallow, she hated that part of the building, but at this point there was no turning back.

They walked pass the courtyard, entering the haunted house building. Krystal stopped dead in her tracks looking pale, Dominoe grabbed her hand. "Is everything OK Krystal?" Her hand was ice cold like she stuck it in an ice chest, goosebumps were running up Krystal's arm. "There is a nun present her name is Pam, she has my hand right now and is going to guide us through the haunted house safely." Dominoe was freaked out,

Pam was the nun that committed suicide off the top of the building she read about and who she has been seeing. Krystal began to walk as Pam was guiding her through the haunted house. They went through the guillotine scene, into the vampire cave, the hillbilly shack, the kitchen, the rag hallway where they stopped again. "I see a little girl at the end of the hall asking to play with us, her name is Kelly." The little girl that died in the school, Dominoe thought to herself. Was she dreaming now or was this really happening? They began to walk again into the psycho ward scene, the electric chair, then they entered the part that people have claimed to not want to be alone in that was located towards the back of the haunted house. It started with the entrance of the mummy scene, Krystal gasped and stopped before they can enter. "Pam left me and ran off, but there is a military black man in front of me, he's very angry and yelling at us that he wants us out of the building now." Everyone started to panic as the candle went out on its own and a cold shock of electricity ran through their bodies. They all ran out the mummy scene into the emergency hallway back to the casting room. Krystal sat on the sofa, breathing in and out, she gasped again looking up. "What is it Krystal?" Dominoe asked. "He's here in the room with us, he followed us and is in rage, demanding we leave this building immediately and never return."

She ran out the door before anyone, Dale left to chase her. Dominoe and Ms. Candie looked around the room, seeing nothing. Ms. Candie screamed out loud running out the door and falling forward on the concrete ground. She was in panic; Krystal and dale were in the corner outside silent. Dominoe helped Ms. Candie up. "Ms. Candie are you OK?" "I felt a burn on my back like fire." They raised her shirt up and branded into her skin was a fresh long red scratch going across her back. The negative energy, the nun, little girl, military man, she did not want to admit it, but all the happenings, the sightings, the stories. Not fiction, but one hundred percent fact and she was not dreaming, she was living everything as real as it can be. Ms. Candie was so frightened she agreed to still stay and work for the haunted house, but never again would she go through the haunted house itself. She will stay in the casting area overseeing and send someone in the back if need be. Ms. Candie locked the door leaving in her car without turning around. "Are you two alright?" "I'm fine, it's my sister, I've never seen her react like this before. There is evil in that building, you must stay away from there, everyone must stay away." "That's impossible, it's a haunted house attraction that opens in just a week, there's no way I will keep anyone away." Krystal got up from the ground, placing her right hand over Dominoes shoulder. "It's what he wants, not everyone else, no harm done if no one enters and if they do, God have mercy on their soul." "Wait how do we get rid of them?" Dominoe asked. "I have done many cases, but this one was the most negative I ever encountered. I think there is no way unless you demolish the school where the spirits have no choice but to try and free themselves. I have no answers, it's just too much and to risky, I'm sorry Dominoe."

Krystal and Dale jumped into their silver jeep and drove off. Dominoe had no closure, still questions and still a fear of being on these grounds. It was time to start looking for a job elsewhere before she gets hurt even worse, killed. She began heading back to her car, looking up again seeing Pam looking down at her through the window. This time the nun intelligently responded to her by waving at her, Dominoe began to cry as she waved back wiping the tears off her cheek. Dominoe felt all the emotions from the nun, something she couldn't explain and never felt before.

Chapter 26

Dominoe left the school passing a church on her street, looking at it in her rear mirror. She pulled to the side taking deep breaths, seeing an empty plastic bottle on the walkway with the cap on it still. She grabbed the bottle and turned her car around parking at the church. She walked inside the church looking up at the cross. "Forgive me father for what I'm about to do, but I need some kind of protection." She pulled out the plastic bottle and began to pour some holy water in it, she then gave the sign of the cross while exiting out the building.

She pulled up to her house, in disbelief as she entered her house at what she just did. She immediately called Liz but got her answering machine. "Hi Liz, its Dominoe, I did it, I had the medium come today. I believe in everything what I am seeing, she proved enough to make me believe it. I really don't want to believe it, but what choice do I have when the facts are in front of you? There is closure with my belief, but none of getting the spirits out the school. Anyway, I'm not going to keep on with this subject I also want to know how you are feeling? Give me a call back as soon as you can, I love you." Dominoe hung the phone up in tears, hoping she will hear her cousin's voice again and hope she went to work Monday and the school was destroyed by a tornado or something.

She got into the shower and heard a loud noise from the living room. She turned the water off rushing into the living room. "Hello?" She looked around the room, seeing nothing unusual until her bare wet feet hit the books from the library. They were scattered on the ground like they were thrown off the table. Whatever was attached to her, was making it known at her home. She ran to her bedroom, grabbing the bottle of holy water and began sprinkling it everywhere in the house while reciting a prayer. She was not alone, no matter where she was, not even her own house.

Chapter 27

Monday morning was back and Dominoe still showed up. All she can do now is try to ignore all happenings as best as she can and if all fails, start praying, that was her only weapon. She could not quit her job yet, finding a new one first was a priority. She sat in her office twirling her pencil in her hair, a fragrance smell of perfume floated in the air, she just placed her head down and ignored it.

The day was finished as she waited for all the teachers and students to leave so she can pull out the holy water from her purse and bless everything. She went around every room sprinkling holy water and reciting back. "Bless this school, take away all negative energy from us and fill it with all positive energy, fill these walls with love and peace." She made her rounds through the whole first part of the building then decided her faith and went into the haunted house part.

She paused in front of the entrance to the cast room. "Dominoe Breaux what are you thinking?" She said to herself while staring at the doorknob. "Faith Dominoe, faith." She said as she opened the door, with the smell of fresh cut wood and paint entering her nose. There were workers inside working on their tight schedule of opening in just a week. She went around them when they were not looking reciting the words she was using and sprinkling holy water. She walked through a little of the first part of the haunt, blessing it, she got to the middle and stopped.

She heard a ball bouncing from the hallway, she walked in the middle of the hallway staring at a little girl with a ball on the ground staring back at her. "Please lady can you come play with me?" She closed her eyes and began praying, the little girl disappeared when her eyes opened back. She stopped at where they left from the other day with the medium, taking a deep breath, closing her eyes for a second.

She began to walk through blessing and repeating the praying words. When she got to the clown room, she heard a loud bang like a two by four falling against something. She jumped up yelling back. "If there is anything negative in here I'm asking you nicely to please go away, we don't want you here!" No sound as she went on and was last left in the dark black wall maze sprinkling holy water and reciting her words.

She was in the middle of the maze hearing a click noise and the lights going out. All she can see is pitch black in front of her as she began to panic feeling of the walls for direction. She screamed for help running and bumping into walls trying to find her way out. She started to feel light headed and taking deep breaths as she heard a growl from behind her ear like a dog. She screamed out loud running faster into a wall falling down to the hard-dark gray concrete ground. Her eyes became heavy as she saw nothing, last thing she can remember is that growl again before fading into a deep sleep.

Chapter 28

Dominoe awoke with the feeling of a cold rag on top her head. Her eyes opened surrounded by volunteer workers of the haunted house. "Are you ok Ms. Dominoe?" One of them said from a small distance, as she regained her sight and raised her head up only to lay it back down feeling a small pain in her head. She hit the wall so hard it knocked her out cold and left a big blue bruise on the top right of her forehead. "Do you need us to call an ambulance Ms. Dominoe?" "I'm fine, I just need to lay here for a little bit."

She finally got the energy to get up looking around to see the group explaining to them what happened. One of them suggested it could have been one of them as they were heading back to the front but did not know anyone was in the maze. She knew it wasn't human whatever the noise was., from that day the maze was off limits when the haunt is not open, unless work is being done inside of it. "I think I can walk out of here now; thank you guys you are all great volunteers."

They all waved bye to her as she exits the building, she looked up at the window for the nun to wave but saw nothing.

Dominoe left for home still in pain, not the best condition to drive, but decided to anyway.

She got home heading straight to the shower, then took two pills of pain medicine before resting her head in bed. She fell asleep awaking in the middle of the night, an urge came through her to look at the photos one more time on the internet. She searched for pictures of Hope Institute, she saw the pictures of Pam and Kelly. She had seen them with her own eyes, she wishes she knew them more and that they never felt pain like they did.

She went into her bottom cabinet in the kitchen not much a drinker but kept alcohol just in case a drink was needed. She poured her flavored vodka into a small glass with two ice cubes and drank it straight. She was a mix drink girl but was in the mood for a straight drink. She gulped her vodka, feeling a buzz, returning to her room laying back down in her warm bed sprawled out. She read about hiring help like voodoo and hoodoo queens to get rid of negative energy from places, but after what happened from the medium she decided it was too risky and too costly. All she can do was pray and take matters into her own hands.

Chapter 29

Dominoe entered her office the next day with the smell of alcohol under her breathe buried in her coffee. Her head was spinning even more from both the bump and the alcohol. Ms. Maria came in to show her the funding's for next semester and changes being made. She just grabbed the papers and said thank you pretending like she cared and knew what was going on.

Her eyes started to roll deeper into sleep, they were wide open with the shining light that startled her. A shiny white orb about the size of a baseball bouncing through the hallway. She got up to follow it, but it disappeared into a closet in one of the storage rooms. She opened the closet door slowly and hesitant thinking it may be some kind of mystery inside. Inside she found empty boxes and a shoe box, she flipped through the boxes, finding nothing but old grade charts and papers from students. She stared at the shoe box with a suspicious gut feeling, slowly hesitant to open it like a bomb was inside. She pulled out a small jar of perfume that had a sexy fruit mist smell to it. It was the same fragrance smell she smelled before inside the school, on side of the perfume was a Christmas card dating back to 1963 that read.

"My darling Elizabeth, it is hard not being able to spend Christmas with you. It is a nightmare here and very hard to outlive, but you are what keeps me going. I wish I can be there to give you a gift in person and the life you deserve. So here is a little something I picked up, I have some sprayed on your picture so that I can smell you and think of you anytime."

Love Jonathan.

It was a gift for the lady who ran this school once and was considered mean dying in the hands of her crazy husband. She felt a cold breeze pass through her curly blonde hair, standing up slowly as the stack of boxes fell with force. She backed up gasping, staring at the boxes on the ground, running out of there. Dominoe felt a rage inside of her, fear that it was a negative energy trying to control her, she ran outside with the perfume in her hand, throwing it at the concrete white wall, smashing it to pieces. She stared at the dirty white wall stained with purple perfume running down to the ground, she smirked at the broken glass. "Take that." She said quietly under her tongue

Chapter 30

It was lunch time on a Thursday, one day to the opening of the haunted house season. Dominoe felt like the school itself was a haunted house and a world of hell. Her cousin Liz was getting worse with the cancer; she has lost more weight since the last time seeing her. She would just sit quietly into space not smiling, just a cold look in her eyes like she is ready. Her parents don't talk to her no more, Dominoe does not know the reason till this day. Her friends don't talk much to her no more, Dominoe was the only thing close to her.

Dominoe had heard of another haunted house commercial on the radio. Them and Bloodstone Institute go against each other every year for the top in the city. The other haunt was the house of horror done at a fire station. The Co-owner of that place Kenny Brentwood worked here for years but quit cause of creative differences. The two haunts are said to be big competition for the West bank and are both equally the same cost, ten dollars a person to get in and fifteen for V.I.P. or as Bloodstone Institute called it V.I.V., very important victim.

Ms. Maria walked into Dominoes office with a box. "I am

so sorry to barge in like this, but I need to run to the bathroom so bad and the volunteers need this ASAP. Can you please run this to them for me?" Dominoe was annoyed on the inside, trying to get away from that evil place, but can never seem to find a way to. "Sure," she said annoyingly. "Thank you so much." Ms. Maria ran out the office like a bat out of hell. The box was cut open, she decided to take a sneak peek at what she must risk her pulse for. Inside was the new seasons shirts, they had a reaper in the middle with all kinds of random characters surrounding it. On the back of the shirt was a tag line that read. "We'll scare the hell out of you." The tag line seemed a little vulgar for the public but was no concern of hers.

She picked up the box exiting the building, walking close to the blessed Mary statue where the graveyard scene was surrounding her. It all just seemed so wrong but couldn't do nothing about it. She saw volunteers from the distance, making a scene, Mongo came from his car right by Dominoe as they both ran to see what was going on. They got there to see old man Clements on the ground having a heart attack. Dominoe dropped the box and onto her knees. "Quick someone call 911!" She cried. "It's going to be OK, just hang in there." Old man Clements grabbed Dominoe by the shoulder, pulling her close to him whispering. "I saw him; I saw the son of a bitch. He's so evil, my heart is too weak for this place, get away from here as soon as you can child."

He stopped breathing laying still with his eyes open, no pulse, no deep breaths, just dead in the middle of the concrete. The silence and tears surrounded his body with surprising faces, no one never saw it coming. Dominoe cried on his chest, not knowing him too well, but knew he was full of kindness. The thought of dying here and your soul never leaving this building, to be tortured by a spirit named Jonathan and never escape. That was a nightmare no person should face, Dominoe was not going to be stuck in that nightmare.

Chapter 31

Everybody heard the echo from the ambulance surrounding old man Clements body. Ms. Candie was taking it the hardest, knowing him since a child, everybody else just sat in silence with their heads down praying. The ambulance arrived to pick up his body, all the volunteers stared at his covering body as they placed him inside and left. Everyone around her was not safe, all these poor souls around her not part of the curse but affected by this energy that runs through the building.

    Ms. Maria tapped Dominoe on the shoulder. "Can I see you in my office, please?" What did she want? For the first time Dominoe was not afraid if it was her losing her job. They sat down in the office, Ms. Maria looked scared staring out the window. "You know what's really going on here, don't you?" Dominoe looked confused. "What do you mean Ms. Maria?" "There have been things happening here for a long time, me and others have all experienced it. We just don't talk about it, so we don't chase away people and mark the school with another story, it doesn't need. Plus, I will tell you something that doesn't leave this room." "Sure Ms. Maria." "There have been rumors that the school was built on a burial ground, no one has never been able to prove it, but wouldn't surprise me." Dominoe was in shock of this news, she never saw it anywhere while researching the school or even thought of the idea. "You've experienced things out of the ordinary, too haven't you?" Dominoe took a breath feeling some relief. "Yes ma'am, I have, since day one." "This school is hard to keep employees and it's getting worse to even keep anyone alive, we have asked request to move the school so many times, but they refuse. This is the only job I have, I've tried many times to get out, but no one would call back, my advice to you Dominoe if you can, get out. Your young and have many years to look forward to, me I have some, most my life has passed. I don't want to see you go or anything bad to happen to you, because you really are doing a good job here, but it's just not fair to keep you imprison in this hell. I'll even recommend you if anything comes up, your too smart to be here." "Thank you Ms. Maria I appreciate that." Dominoe got up from her seat and shook Ms. Maria's hand, walking out the office relieved and was not alone here. The day was done she grabbed her things to walk out of the building. She saw volunteers being dropped off by parents and others parking themselves for dress rehearsal the eve before they open. It was Halloween around the corner her least favorite holiday and was going to be surrounded by it even more for a month. She got into her car to head home, it was the first time she saw a person die in front of her. All other family members were already prepped in their casket. With her cousin on the verge of death, she doesn't know how she will handle that when the time comes.

It was late and windy outside with a low chance for rain. Dominoe sat in her living room in the dark watching old black and white movies while sipping on wine. She started to doze off when her home phone rang. "Hello." "Dominoe its Liz." She was happy to hear her cousin's voice but was worried about her breathing and silence on the other end. "Liz?" "I'm inside the haunted house Dominoe." She raised up from the sofa in shock. "You're what?" "I'm inside the haunted house, I broke in. Don't worry it's been closed for an hour now. I can't take it anymore cousin, the pain, the future I am going to end it all tonight for good. I'm going to do it here, this place has cursed me for the last time, it wants me so bad, it can have me." "Liz wait!" "Goodbye

Dominoe, I love you." She hung up as Dominoe cried out her name repeatedly, trying to call her back, but no answer. She grabbed a pair of jeans and slipped on her shoes running to her car through the heavy wind nearly knocking her to the ground. She backed out the driveway fast driving there not knowing what to expect or see when she gets there.

Chapter 32

Lightning struck from the distance, her car was being pushed back and forth from the heavy wind. The thought of finding her cousin's dead body in the place was running through her head. She arrived at the haunted house terrified for her life but would do anything for her cousin. The exterior was pitch black, it looked like the devil himself was covering the exterior buildings.

She saw the lock broken off at the haunted house door entrance. She took a big deep breath opening the door and entering. The inside haunt lights were all turned on, all she can see was strobe lights reflecting on the wall, black, red and green lights exposing the sets as she walked through searching. She started to call Liz's name out hoping she would yell back. She walked deep into the haunted house that everyone feared. "Liz, where are you?" "I'm over here." She heard from a soft-spoken voice as she flashed her light on the corner where Liz was sitting Indian style with a pistol in her hand.

She looked up at Dominoe while spinning the gun on the ground. "Liz where did you get that?" "Doesn't matter, what matters is that your here with me for my last words and peace."

"Liz don't talk like that; you don't want to do this." "My parents abandoned me cause of all their money I spent on drugs, hanging out with that asshole Freddy. He ruined my life and is the reason why I am dying from cancer right now." Dominoe walked slowly to her. "Calm down Liz and give me the gun." "I loved my parents and loved working here, it was fun, so many friends so many fun times, but one night had to go fuck my whole life up." Liz cocked the gun while picking it up from the ground. "Liz please don't do this." "I'm sorry Dominoe, I'm doomed either way, they ruined me so now they can have me, finishing what the bastards started." "Liz please!" "I love you Domino." She placed the gun in her mouth splattering her brains against the wall. Dominoe fell on her knees paralyzed bursting into tears seeing her cousin's face with blood running down her mouth and her body stiff. Dominoe began to have a panic attack, losing control of her lungs. The school has brought nothing but trouble to her and now to her family. She snapped on the inside barging out of the scene. "No!!" She screamed out as loud as she can, hearing her scream echo throughout the whole haunted house. "You want to destroy people and take someone I love! Well I'm going to destroy the heart and soul of you and see how you like it!" She screamed barging out of the haunted house with an idea in mind.

Chapter 33

She ran across the courtyard beating into the wind. She began to hear echoes of children's voices surrounding her as she was falling from the wind and getting back up. She ran to the shed on the side of the school where old man Clements had his tools and supplies. She found two cans of gasoline, but no lighter, she remembered one of the teachers was a smoker likely to have an extra lighter somewhere in her desk.

She broke the glass of the front door of the school racing up the stairs to the classrooms. She made a mess digging through the classroom until finally finding a lighter. She ran out the classroom running for the stairs. She felt a sharp pain on her back out of nowhere and a shove knocking her down the stairs. Her back had a red scratch mark like Ms. Candie, she used her arm to get up, but fell right back down feeling the pain from her shoulder.

She grabbed both cans of gasoline, screaming in pain from the pressure of her broken shoulder. The entrance door of the school slammed open, breaking the glass windows, she turned around exiting through the back door running as fast as she can to the other building, tripping twice on the way there. She screamed of her shoulder pain getting close to the other building.

She kicked the door storming in, pouring gasoline all over the place. She found the paint room, grabbing paint thinner and started to pour it all over the walls and sets. She went back to the cast room to grab the other can of gasoline, startled as she looked up, seeing Pam and Kelly's spirit stare at her. "What are you doing Ms.?" The little girl cried. "I'm ending this and freeing Y'all." "No, you don't want to do that, you will make him mad," Pam cried. "Soon he won't be able to do anything." Dominoe said as she kept pouring and pouring gasoline all over the place. She flew back from a push into a wall with a screw sticking out that jabbed right into her back. She pulled her body forward slowly as the rusted screw came out with blood pouring out of her.

She walked back towards the cast room with blood from her back dripping on the ground. She heard from behind in a raging voice. "You can't do this; I want you out of here now!" She kept running not looking back, knowing that it was Jonathan yelling and demanding her to leave. Bricks and two by fours began to fly hitting her, causing bruises and cuts on her.

By the time she got to the back of the haunt her face and back was a bloody mess. She poured the remaining gasoline in the clown scene and ran out of there being pushed against the wall in the mummy scene. She saw a dirty haunted house shirt laying on the ground by her hand. She heard thumping from behind like a soldier marching towards her. She turned around staring face to face with a full apparition of a bloody Jonathan and Sister Elizabeth. "Why are Y'all doing this to this place? Just leave, nobody wants your negative energy here!" Jonathan got closer to Dominoes face, blood dripping from his open wound on his neck. "Because I am the one who started this here and I'm the one who is going to finish it." "Not if I do it first," Dominoe replied. Sister Elizabeth walked up to Dominoe. "Child you can't win with him, just give it up and let him take your soul, fighting will only make it worse." Jonathan yelled in rage at Sister Elizabeth. "You stay out of this, she's mine." Sister Elizabeth turned around "You are forgetting one thing, honey, I made you here." Sister Elizabeth grabbed Jonathan holding him back. "Run child, run while I have him before it's too late! Run!" Is all

Dominoe heard echoing as she ran into the cast room with the dirty shirt in her hand.

She ran out the door, pulling out the lighter, lighting the shirt on fire. She raised the shirt to throw it inside, but paused as she saw an apparition of Liz, Sister Pam and Kelly standing next to each other looking at her from inside. Liz looked at her. "Do it Dominoe, now." "I love you Liz," she said throwing her bad shoulder back in pain throwing the flaming shirt inside the building as it roared into flames. "That's for my cousin you bastard's!" She heard loud alien like screams coming from the flames, sounded like souls being burned alive.

She ran back to the car covered in blood, turning the key to drive off, not even looking back at the flaming buildings being burned to the ground. She had no care about the building or the negative souls all she can think about was Liz and the positive energies. She hoped they were finally free to move forward into the afterlife forgetting about the past.

Dominoe made it to the hospital a bloody mess like a scene from Texas chainsaw. The doctors rushed her to the back, cleaning her and stitching all the open wounds. She stayed in the hospital for two weeks, never telling a soul about what happened that blazing night. Her excuse for all the blood and cuts was being attacked in the city while the man escaped. It was the best excuse she can come up with, it was better than, "I was attacked by evil spirits and watched my cousin commit suicide." The cops seemed suspicious, but the nightmare was over and that's all that counted.

On her last day she saw a full apparition form of Liz, Kelly and Pam at the foot of her hospital bed. They thanked her for freeing them, acknowledging her that they will be alright and will not suffer any longer. Dominoe laid back with a smile, she was out of a job, but helped souls move on to the afterlife. It was one of the best accomplishments she could have ever done, now she can start all over as a survivor.

Bloodstone Institute was no more, but the stories were forever. Those affected by the weird happenings and deaths can now move on and not speak of their tales, unless they want to. Everybody was free, and a new chapter begins, hopefully for the future of the kids can continue without a doubt. Hell had officially frozen over, and the lost souls were finally lifted from the ground, into a much better place.

Epilogue

After the school burned down the savings account was full of years savings thanks to the haunted attraction. The archdiocese finally after decades decided to use it to relocate the school and start from scratch, finding a good piece of land not part of a burial tribe and rebuild it from top to bottom. They wanted to forget the name Hope Institute, that name caused more misery and harm to others than anyone can imagine. They did some research and thought of local customs, until finally coming up with the name Chinchuba Institute. It came from a Choctaw tribe name, in Choctaw Chinchuba means alligator. Thinking of the local scene, alligators are a common animal surrounding the swamps, alligators have no hearing in their ears, since it was a school for the deaf, the name fitted the theme well.

Dominoe tried finding a new position right after the building burned down, she was hesitant, but stayed on for a few years in her same position. They moved to a smaller area while the new building was being constructed and gave her a pay bump to stay with them. No crazy events happened at the new location, no spirits followed them from the old building. Dominoe eventually got married, she met her husband at her local church. They dated for two years, married with two children, she named her first child Liz after her late cousin. Her second child Jeff came a year later; it was like holding on to a piece of heaven in her arms.

Dominoe later became a head of education for the school system, she stayed in that position until she retired. Dominoe never told her family or friends about what happened that dreadful time at Hope Institute. The story was never brought up by surprise and she tried her best to never think about it. Her Cousin Liz's spirit followed her around, she knew it was her, but did not mind it. She considered her a guardian angel watching over her. Her future was all she ever thought of and loved. She had a happy life with ups and downs, but now when her time comes, she has done everything she wanted and can go in peace with no regrets.

ABOUT THE AUTHOR

David Dugas Jr lives ten minutes outside of New Orleans with his wife Erica. He has had an imagination since childhood, utilizing it to his best skills. He grew up wanting to be a filmmaker but fell off that dream after many years. He began story writing back in 2010, just months before his mom passed away with cancer. It was a way to keep his mind off what was happening and a beginning of a new chapter in his life of using his imaginative skills. It helped get by even after her death, he has been writing as often as possible, trying to share his work to the world of readers. His other hobbies are watching movies, anything Disney related, reading, paranormal investigating, haunted housing and anything else horror related. You can contact him on his facebook page, www.facebook.com/daviddugasjrauthor. His wattpad username ddugas for his free short stories. Email him at ddugas1986@gmail.com. And tweet him at @ddugasjrauthor.

Instagram: Zombhorror

Made in the USA
Columbia, SC
21 May 2018